I0621828

BECOMING

A

HERO

C.R. GARMEN

Becoming a Hero

Copyright © 2019 by C.R. Garmen

All rights reserved.

No part of this book may be reproduced in any form or by any means without the prior written consent of the author, excepting brief quotes used in reviews.

Please do not participate in or encourage piracy of copyrighted materials in violation of the author's rights. Purchase only authorized editions.

This is a work of fiction. Names, characters, places, events and incidents either are the product of the author's imagination or are used fictitiously, and any resemblance to persons, living or dead, business establishments, events or locales is entirely coincidental.

To the extent that the image or images on the cover of this book depict a person or persons, such person or persons are merely models and are not intended to portray any character or characters featured in the book.

Interior Design: RMGraphX

ISBN 978-1-7337463-1-1

BECOMING
A
HERO

C.R. GARMEN

AUTHOR'S NOTE

This story was previously published as The Lost Kingdom, in the Rise of the Fallen anthology, by Trinity Author Services. Becoming A Hero is an expanded edition of the short story with an alternate ending.

The inspiration for both stories came from a Dungeons and Dragons campaign that I had participated in. Our group was made of a bunch of mismatched heroes who had the oddest quirks and used their unique abilities to try and stop the world from becoming worse than it already was. I would say the goal was to save the world from evil, but unfortunately, we never made it that far. One character in particular sparked the idea for Paul Paulson. The character, who was played by a dear friend of mine, was a dwarf who only fought with common household objects. He was hysterical but not the best warrior around. As my friend said, "it takes more than a sword to win a fight."

So, this book is for everyone who isn't a natural born warrior. To the people that work hard to see something through even when everything else is fighting against them. You don't have to be anything other than yourself to become a hero.

ACKNOWLEDGEMENTS

Thank you to everyone who has helped me bring this fun tale to life. I would list you all by name, but that would be a book within itself. I'm truly blessed to have such a large and encouraging support system both in person and online. I can't tell you all how much it touches me, and how much I appreciate that push you all give for me to follow my dreams. Without you all, this may never have happened.

Special shout out to my fur and scale babies for being amazing.

CHAPTER ONE

"GOOD JOB, GILBERT!" I praised my trusty short-haired, grey donkey as he steadily climbed the slope of Forbidden Mountain. Making the trek with the slow animal somehow seemed ominous, but this route was the quickest way to get back to Terragon from Melford. To be frank, I assumed the name was a warning of the treacherous terrain, rather than a rule one must follow as set forth by the Seven Kings. I had used that road many times during my life to trade handcrafted pots and pans and had never encountered any issues.

The cart jumped and jostled as the old wooden wheels hit a hole on the path. I gritted my teeth at the sound of the goods clattering together in the back. The biggest threat to our journey would be if the cart finally gave out after ten years of rolling. Well, the other concern was my pet donkey having a heart attack. I narrowed my eyes as Gilbert stopped to sniff a rock.

He was an old man in donkey years, but I couldn't afford a younger, stronger, or smarter animal.

"Gilbert, let's go! You can sniff strange things all you want when we get home!" I cracked the reins, and Gilbert let out a long bray of defiance. Stubborn thing. Pebbles fell from farther up the mountain. I squinted against the harsh midday sun to see what had shaken them free. Nothing. Figures. "I should have learned to be a butcher," I groused as I snapped the reins again. While I enjoyed making beautiful and super durable pots and pans, the work didn't exactly pay well. That year, in particular, had been rather dry. A career choice of selling beef or pork would have been easier. Butchers were always needed. Plus, the hard work of catching the animals was done for them by the hunters. Or their pigs and cows were raised in fields nearby.

Gilbert was delaying our travels again with another bray of concern. I frowned at my steed, but before I could get him moving another couple of inches, more rocks slid from a cliff above us. Goosebumps covered my arms, the hair on the back of my neck stood on end, and I wiped sweat off my brow. The old donkey seemed to study me as I tried to shake off the sensation of being watched. Maybe the shifting earth was something after all...

Gilbert shuddered and reared back, nearly knocking into me. I yanked on the reins and leaned forward in my seat as the cart threatened to tip over. While we steadied ourselves, I scowled at my companion and barked out, "Now what's wrong with you?"

That was when they appeared.

Four large men, armed with knives and cold smiles, slunk out from behind massive boulders and long cracks in the mountainside. Gilbert jerked against his reins again and brayed out a chorus of displeasure.

The edge of the mountain where we stood frozen in fear was narrow, with a sharp drop off, and the bottom wasn't even visible from this height. If Gilbert didn't calm down soon, the cart would tip over, and we would both die. I swallowed against my building terror and eyed the men as they slyly approached us.

"Y-you're not really this stupid, right? One wr-rong move from any of us and we'll all f-fall to our deaths!" I stuttered.

"Who said we were going to fall with you?" One of them snarled back. "Just toss over your gold, and we'll let you pass."

Starve to death because I'd be broke, or fall? The options were tough. I carefully slid one hand down to the side where my knife was sheathed. I'd never used it for self-defense before, but I believed there was a first time for everything, even if I was scared out of my mind. Pulling the small blade from its sheath, I took a deep breath and raised the weapon in front of myself. "I'll give you all one more chance to leave, or I shall have to take your lives," I stated, silently proud of myself for keeping my voice steady.

One of the thieves, a man with a wicked scar crossing over his left eye, laughed. "And who are you?"

I narrowed my eyes. "I am Paul Paulson the third by name. If you haven't heard of me yet, then count yourself lucky."

"I think we'll take our chances." The man with the scar hissed as he spoke, drawing out his own crooked blade and swiping it through the air. Gilbert reared back again, kicking his front legs with a shriek of protest. I cried out for him to stop as he wildly kicked at the enemy, jerking the cart in the process and nearly bucking me out of my seat. The reins dropped onto the wooden floor and as I bent to grab them, the cart started forward, then tipped left. I glanced up long enough to watch as Gilbert scrambled to find purchase on the uneven ground while slowly slipping off the side of the mountain. My heart dropped.

And then, so did we.

My mind couldn't handle the concept of facing certain death. The images around me suddenly snapped into a sharp focus and slowed to a crawl. Gilbert's face appeared terror-struck as he silently screamed for help while pulling the cart slowly off the side of the cliff. The jaws on the thieves all dropped in shock as they watched the wheels slip one by one into the cold, blustering winds. Momentarily, I even saw myself twist toward the safety of the mountain with a hand outstretched, as if I thought I could grab hold of something magical to save us. The knife I'd gripped had become forgotten, dropped into the endless void of clouds beneath us. My trousers were soaked.

My head spun as time seemed to disappear in a flash. My screams, and those of my favorite donkey, reverberated across the sky. Without thought, I latched onto the wooden bar of the cart and sucked in a deep breath as we plummeted downward. My bottom left the cart seat and soon I found myself hanging upside down with Gilbert struggling beside me. I eyed the harness trapping him, almost a foot away from my hips. The buckles slapped wildly in the wind, but undoing them in a free fall would probably take an act of God.

Silver clouds rushed up to greet us, making me temporarily close my eyes as I knew the inevitable was quickly coming our way. I was so far beyond terrified that it took a minute to register a shift in the air. My tunic was no longer swishing behind me but almost floating in the warm breeze. I slowly cracked open my eyes again to see we had been enveloped in sparkling clouds that stretched for miles around us. Our descent had slowed. When the fingers of my left hand uncurled from around the bar and stretched out to my dear old friend, he looked at me, calm with a curious spark to his gaze. Once I was certain I wouldn't lose my grip— nor my arm—from the pain of holding onto a heavy piece of equipment with only one thin limb, I reached back toward Gilbert's buckles. It blew straight into my outstretched hand, seemingly on its own accord. Working quickly, and ignoring the oddity of this entire situation, I released the buckle from its harness. Gilbert was half free! Moving as swiftly and carefully as possible, I slid my way over to reach the other side of my donkey.

The shiny clasp unhooked under my trembling grip. Gilbert tilted his head as the leather strap slid out. I gave him a watery smile. "I hope I am able to see you again on the other side." I thought he nodded in reply as he rose up and away from the cart.

The magic that had seemed to hold me suspended in the sea of clouds suddenly ended, and I found myself tumbling to the ground again. I caught glimpses of luscious, overgrown trees decorating a barren trail next to the mountainside. My stomach seemed to move into my throat, and my lungs were burning. Or maybe that was my heart? It was hard to tell while heading for a crash landing on top of an angry ogre.

An *ogre?*

I blinked and yelped. An ogre with a large club was lumbering directly below us, surrounded by a band of warriors who didn't appear to be fairing so well. Three of them were off to the side, bleeding from gaping wounds across their chests. The rest looked pale as if the fight had been waging for too long and everyone was on their last legs. I might have been wrong, though.

The paleness on their faces could just be their natural coloring. Elves, for example, were known to have very fair skin too.

Something whistled past my ear and shot like a bullet to the ground. As much as I was dreading the impact, I realized that at least my fall would be broken. Were ogres cushy? I knew they were tall, but I hadn't the slightest clue if their bodies were more muscle or fat. Never got close enough to one to tell.

A long time ago, someone told me, "It's not the fall that will kill you, it's the sudden stop at the end…"

What is wrong with me to think of something like that at a time like this?

I closed my eyes and held both arms crossed in front of my face in a weak attempt to protect it. And I prayed.

A soft, wet *thunk* sound met my ears before I collided with something as hard as stone. The breath left my body in a rush, and I coughed to try and regain it. When I landed the creature was still moving. Slowly it toppled from its feet, and I was jarred by the impact of it collapsing on the ground.

A series of gasps echoed around me. I groaned weakly in reply and opened my eyes. Flexing my fingers and toes, I was elated to realize all my body parts seemed to work just fine. Sore, maybe, but I didn't think I'd broken any bones. The gods must have answered my prayers! Which was a first…

I blinked again and slowly slid off the ogre... A patchwork leather vest covered a large, muscular back with green tinted skin. I gave a harsh gulp and scrambled to my feet. The ogre I had landed on had my little dagger lodged in his skull. The wound was bubbling some thick, almost black liquid. My stomach heaved.

I gagged and spun around, searching the immediate area for any traces of a donkey falling from the skies. If, relatively speaking, I'd landed safely; then maybe Gilbert did as well. I would never complain about the poor guy again. Though my view was slightly obstructed by baffled fighters, I couldn't see any grey fur—or hear a tired bray—anywhere.

Damn. Focusing back on the band of warriors who were circled around me, I attentively asked, "Has anyone seen a donkey?" Each face in the crowd was frozen in shock. If I hadn't been feeling so sick, the question would have been funny. Swords clanged to the ground. Arrows were slowly put away. I scrubbed a hand down my face as whispers drifted around me.

Three wounded, and seven standing... Gods, I hated math...

The group was a small army. One of them, a large man at least six feet tall, stepped forward. He had a long, brown beard and a scar that slashed down the right side of his face. His eyes were hard, and his shoulders almost as broad as the ogre who stood before us.

The man was eyeing me, as I was studying him. Maybe something about my appearance made him nod and then burst into laughter. He took two steps forward, swung a meaty arm around my shoulders, and turned back to his band. "It has finally happened! We have found the chosen one!" he boasted.

My legs were ready to give out beneath me, but I was alert enough to look up at the giant and squeak out, "What?"

Either my words never made it up the large hike to his ear, or he was purposely ignoring me because he continued to address the others, "The prophecy is finally coming true!"

I blinked slowly and tilted my head up to face the man who could knock me flat with a simple pat on the back. Not intimidating at all… "Wait, what prophecy? And has anyone seen a donkey?"

He looked down at me as his mouth opened to a wide grin. "He shall come from the skies with a strike so powerful it would lay waste to our enemies in a single blow! It's a prophecy written by our last king's oracle, before the darkness took over and warped our lands. A mighty hero is supposed to rise and lead the rebellion, freeing the innocents from evil's hand! More than fifty years have passed since this was written, but the timing couldn't be better. We need you now more than ever!" The large man paused and scratched his beard. "And I can't say that I have. But we'll certainly keep an eye out for one!"

Did I hit my head when I landed on the ogre? How on earth did this giant associate me falling down a mountainside with saving a kingdom? My eyes slowly focused on the hilt of the knife protruding from the creature's skull, and my stomach flipped again. Sure, I guess it might look that way, but it was an accident. Nobody could honestly believe…

Yet when I lifted my gaze to the small army around me, I saw nothing but hope sparkling in their tired eyes. Smiles started to adorn their faces, and the whispers grew into cheers and praise. I swallowed hard again and opened my mouth. The man shook me with his own joy radiating so brightly it was nearly blinding. "Glad to finally meet you! I'm Aasgard, and I'll be right by your side during this war. It's truly an honor…" he paused, lifting a brow as my mouth flopped open and closed a couple times.

"I'm Paul, but there has to be some sort of mistake. I accidentally fell off the cliffside with my donkey, Gilbert. We need to get back home to make more pots and pans since I lost my load during the fall and all. I'm really not a hero. Honestly, you can ask anyone in my kingdom. I haven't the slightest clue how to fight, and I'm kind of attached to living, so I'd rather not learn," I rambled nervously.

"Slow down, boy. I can't keep up with you. If you're worried about fighting, don't worry. You're off to a great start with the ogre. The seven of us couldn't take him down, but you did so in one shot!" Aasgard was insistent and still wore a wide tooth grin.

"Yeah but…" I protested weakly.

He shook me again. "No need to be so humble! It's truly an honor, Sir Paul! Unfortunately, nobody has been able to leave here since The Crook took over."

"What?"

"Well, there is a barrier that was erected to protect our kingdom during the great war. We didn't have a large army or anything, so the king needed to do something to protect us. But when Hosaku took the throne after the king's death, everything around here started changing. We've tried to get past the barrier, to no avail. It just keeps pushing us back inside. The only way is to break the magic that originally created it."

I licked my lips nervously and looked back up the cliff. "There isn't any other way?"

Aasgard shook his head solemnly. "Trust me. We've tried…"

That still didn't mean I had to be a part of their resistance group. I made pots and pans for a living! Swinging around swords and rushing into battle… Hell, I moved kingdoms away from my home, simply to avoid a small feud that my neighbors had. However, the expression of relief on so many battered faces made me choke on the argumentative words I was thinking. Eventually, I gave up and offered everyone in the group a small, awkward wave.

"Thank you, Paul, for saving us," Aasgard added sincerely.

I took a deep breath and nodded. I was going to have to play hero… for the time being at least.

CHAPTER TWO

A ASGARD AND THE rebels took me back to their camp, almost five miles south of the Forbidden Mountains. Progress was slow because the wounded had to be bandaged and carried, but I was thankful for it. I wasn't used to walking long distances on my own, so my legs didn't move as fast as Aasgard's. True to their words, we searched for Gilbert along the way, but didn't find any trace of him.

"Don't fret too much. Donkeys are smart and resilient creatures. He'll be fine, and I'm sure he'll find his way back to you." Aasgard tried to reassure me, whilst I held on to the hope that he was right.

Their camp was situated in between two small valleys. The grass was dead. Patchwork tents had been erected a few feet away from one another, lined up in rows to fit into the dip of the valley. Several fires were blazing along the center of the camp to feed the group and to offer warmth as the day waned. Everyone was wearing either leather or silver armor and had a weapon by their side. Bows, hammers, short swords, long swords, broadswords, knives, and sickles. I'd never seen such an array of weapons before. Even when I'd visited the local blacksmith, I had never witnessed a variety like that laid out on display… much less armed for an impending war.

Time had taken its toll on each face I passed. The men were dusty, tired, and appeared hopeless. Scars adorned the bare flesh of their throats, arms, and legs. Some had slash marks across their faces, similar to the ones on their leader. At least, I assumed Aasgard was in charge of the group.

He motioned the others to take the wounded men to a faded green tent where the healers were ready to tend to them. Luckily, I didn't sustain any major injuries from my fall, only some bruises and a small scrape on my knee. It was patched up with some cloth and salve, and I was fine to go. The healers gave me a small jar of the creamy mixture and said should I get any more small cuts, the salve would work to cleanse them and speed up the healing process. I tucked it away in my small money pouch, which sadly only contained a few coins. The life of a pots and pans salesman wasn't glamorous.

I was led to the middle of the grounds, which resembled a large bonfire pit with overturned logs around it to seat most of the patrons of the camp. A massive black pot was already simmering on the fire near two women who were tending to its contents. The sweet smell of beef made my stomach rumble. Aasgard grinned. "The feast will be ready shortly. We will have our fill tonight before moving west toward the castle."

"The castle?"

"That's where the orb containing the curse of our lands resides. If we destroy it, the magic barrier will break, and you can return to your home."

"Sounds easy enough," I muttered sarcastically while eyeing the warriors around me.

Another large man joined us on a fallen log. His hair was as black as onyx with steel grey eyes that unsettled me more and more, the longer I gazed into them. He wore a single pauldron on his right shoulder that depicted a lion's head in the middle of the cop. Beyond that, leather was stretched across his broad chest, and a black and green kilt covered his waist. "If it were easy, we wouldn't need an army now, yeah?" He rumbled with a voice deeper than the canyons I had crossed to get to Jipsom.

"Sir Paul, meet Nyx-Ente. He's a crazy bastard, but you needn't worry about your back with him around." Aasgard introduced the man with a toothy grin. "But calm yourself. We have a plan. And it's damned good if I say so myself!"

That was... not exactly reassuring. "What is the plan?"

"The group here will split into two teams. One heads west and goes straight toward the castle while the other follows a more southerly route to approach the back gate. We're the west team. We'll leave at first light and follow the valley to the Hyroll's Forest. Inside is a small village that has been long abandoned. By the time we make it there, it should be night. We'll camp inside the buildings to keep out of sight, then continue through at first light. Outside of the forest is another village. I don't know if anyone resides there, so we'll have to walk around it to avoid unnecessary confrontation. From that point on, it's a straight shot up to the castle doors. We'll wait until the second teams make it into position and then strike all at once."

"Riiight," I drawled, "And what's to stop the guards from hacking us into super tiny pieces?"

"The element of surprise! And explosives!" Aasgard announced with a thundering laugh. He patted me on the back, nearly knocking me off my seat in the process. The man had more strength than he seemed to realize.

"Oh, fantastic," I added weakly. "You are aware that I've only ever held a dagger in my hands, correct?"

Aasgard blinked in reply, making me cringe.

"I haven't the slightest clue about how to wield a sword, and I assume since we're headed into a war, I'll need to do so." My admission should have been enough information to, once again, prove that I was no hero. But no, the insane giant merely laughed at me, clapped my back roughly, and announced that he would gladly do the honors of training me to wield a proper weapon. As for everything else, it certainly wasn't the worst plan I'd ever heard. Nyx-Ente and another stringy man who had joined us, exchanged concerned looks with one another. A queasy feeling filled my stomach as I started to ponder how well the rest of the group would take to Aasgard's declaration of my appearance. But the topic quickly changed from our battle plans to introducing me to the rest of the group. So many names and faces stood before me, and they all started to blur together.

"That's Jorgon and Symol, and here's their cousin Aldron, the second of his name. He was named after his father who led the first battle against The Crook when he came into power."

Was the blonde Symol or Jorgon? I was sure all these tiny details would come back to me when it was important. I thought, for a moment that, perhaps I could call everyone "Buddy." That seemed a lot easier for me. Especially after I was introduced to the Dexlock twins.

By the time we'd made it through the entire camp, the sun was setting. My head was spinning, and the food was ready to eat. The meal was a simple stew made with beef so tender it melted in my mouth and flavorful vegetables. A chunk of bread was handed to everyone. As we all tucked in, Aasgard, with a few of the larger warriors, shared stories about the crazy adventures they'd embarked on, and the battles they'd won. The tales were interesting and a little awe-inspiring. Aasgard spoke of being lost in a cave and finding his way out by following the sound of running water. And how he first discovered the lines of the barrier and attempted to smash his way through it, only to have his arm broken in the process.

This army might not be as large as a king's army, but it was easy to see the friendship and loyalty that bound them. I thought that was worth more than numbers alone. Nobody in this group was likely to leave a comrade behind. One member of the troop even gave me a new dagger, a short sword, and a leather vest for protection. A few practice swings of the sword almost resulted in gutting Aldron. Or maybe it was Jorgon. Thankfully I missed, and whoever it was didn't hold any ill will against me for the blunder.

"You need to widen your stance, boy! Shoulders back and eyes forward. Never look away from the enemy," Aasgard coached while my opponent rolled his shoulders.

We got back into our positions and lunged.

"Tighten your grip on the hilt or else you'll be dis—" Oops, too late. My blade was knocked clean out of my hand and plummeted to the ground about three feet behind me.

I groaned and ignored the cocky smirks of the

watchers as I retrieved the sword in question.

"Okay, well… Now you know better. So, get back into position and try it again," Aasgard commanded from the sidelines.

Sweat was pouring down my face as time and time again I faced off against the patient warriors within the camp. My body ached in places I never knew existed, and I was about ready to cry with exhaustion from their ruthless training. The drills didn't stop until well past sunset. And despite my complaints, of which I had many, for the first time in my life, it felt as though I belonged to something.

Since the passing of my parents, I had kept to myself with only Gilbert as my constant companion. Being part of this group was entirely different and sort of, in an insane way, welcoming. If anyone had any doubts about me being a supposed hero, they kept the comments to themselves and helped me learn how to parry and strike. As we all settled into our thin sleeping bags for the night, that thought kept me warm and helped me find a sweet, blissful sleep.

CHAPTER THREE

THE NEXT MORNING, the group prepared to leave. In two hours the fires were put out, everyone's belongings had been gathered, and tents were disassembled and packed away. Honestly, as much as I tried to help, it seemed as if I was simply in the way. Each member had a specific, yet unspoken, task to complete and worked quickly to do so. I was left floundering with the reassurance that I could stand guard while they finished. I saw a bunny grazing while I walked the perimeter, but that was it.

Once everyone had completed their tasks, we separated into our two assigned teams and hit the trail. Each group consisted of approximately forty people, with Aasgard and Nyx-Ente taking the lead for ours. I kept close to the front, more out of curiosity than anything else. Plus, I figured, if anything jumped out to attack us, my best chance for survival was staying near all the big guys.

The day was warm with a soft breeze blowing in from the east. I took a deep breath of fresh air and let it loosen some of my tensed muscles. The journey was surreal. There I was, a young man from a small village with a very ordinary job, joining a resistance to free a lost and forgotten kingdom from sheer demise. Nobody would believe this back home—if I spoke to any of them regularly. I occasionally offered the generic, "Hi, how are you?" but the conversation was kept polite and ended abruptly. Gilbert would shake his head when I told him about this crazy adventure... once we found him, of course.

Large birds circled in the clear, blue sky above us, breaking me out of my reverie. I tensed up while the archers in the back readied their bows. Everyone around me kept their eyes on the creatures while carefully proceeding forward. "Quiet now, those beasts belong to The Crook," Aasgard whispered.

"Beasts? Aren't they just vultures?" I asked, squinting against the sun. One dove closer, revealing long, torn bat wings and a sharp, hooked beak.

"Nay, they aren't vultures anymore. When the new ruler took over, the creatures in our lands started changing. That one is big enough to pick me up and take me to its roost without breaking a sweat."

I swallowed hard. "So why aren't we shooting them down?"

Aasgard grimaced." They are too far away."

21

I was too busy looking up to see the donkey grazing in the field across from us until it neighed. I blinked. Surely, I was mistaken. The little guy brayed in greeting again and began an awkward gallop toward us. "Gilbert!"

Winged demons barreled down from the skies. My eyes grew wide as I watched them dive for my best friend. I ran out toward Gilbert without a second thought. Voices cried out behind me, and a volley of arrows soared overhead. The creatures let out ear-piercing screeches and uncurled their talons. Gilbert sounded a distressed bray as he attempted to dodge them, but he was too slow.

The creatures snagged my donkey and flew back into the skies with the volley of arrows only grazing their skin and landing harmlessly on the ground.

Gilbert screamed, and I think I did too. Our reactions were hard to hear over the sound of my crashing heart. My poor old Gilbert survived the fall down the mountain, only to be ensnared by such a foul beast.

"Oh gods, no!"

Aasgard and Nyx-Ente grabbed my arms and dragged me back toward the army. I didn't fight them. There wasn't any point. Gilbert was gone…

"Those things roost in the castle, lad. Do ya hear me? They roost in the castle's towers!"

I blinked slowly and turned my head to Nyx-Ente. "What?"

"Yer donkey may live yet. Those beasts keep their hoard till they're hungry. Could be days before they decide to eat. If we keep pressin' forward, we'll get to the castle in time to save yer pet."

"Gilbert could still be alive?" I pleaded, desperately seeking out a glimmer of hope.

Aasgard looked at Nyx-Ente with a hardened expression. "Yes, we can still save your Gilbert."

"How do you know this?"

Nyx-Ente turned away from me and sauntered over to speak with some of the archers. I furrowed my brows as I looked to Aasgard for an explanation. He sighed heavily and ran a hand through his beard. "They don't only eat animals. They eat any living creature they can pick up." He paused to look back at Nyx-Ente. "Like little daughters and a beautiful pregnant wife."

My stomach dropped. I closed my eyes against the horror and dread that filled me. "What happened?"

"Nyx-Ente chased them down for three days. When he broke into the castle and snuck up to the top of the towers, he found them being devoured by the creatures—screaming to be saved—while The Evil One watched from the other side of the room, laughing with a goblet filled with wine. I don't know what happened next. We found Nyx-Ente outside the castle walls, a broken shell of a man. I won't press him for any more details. I don't think I would want to know, even if he were willing to tell me."

I nodded in understanding. "And you?" I asked quietly. Aasgard regarded me silently for a moment before letting out another heavy sigh.

"I used to be a farmer. When The Crook took over, he raised the taxes of everyone in the kingdom. It caused many of us to go broke. We held a meeting to discuss how the taxes were gutting families, but The Crook didn't care and told the guards to shut the gate on us. Then, he started sending out those guards to arrest families who couldn't make the monthly taxes. My neighbors started disappearing quickly. I don't know what happened to them, but once I ran out of money, I decided to run. It might not be the most heartbreaking story, but after hearing Nyx-Ente's, I can't help but wonder if the arrested were fed to his disgusting pets. The castle never expanded. Dozens had been taken in. Surely, they couldn't all fit in the cells, so, where are they?"

Aasgard stopped and scratched his beard again.

"That's why that villainous scumbag has to be stopped. He unleashed hellish creatures upon us and ripped families apart with his unquenchable greed. He also keeps us imprisoned within the barrier. If we don't stop him soon, nobody will be around to revolt against him again."

My eyes stung with unshed tears. Licking my lips and clearing my throat, I said, "Let's go," and headed back to the rest of our small army.

It was nearly dusk by the time we had made it to the forest's edge. Everyone in our group exchanged uncertain glances with each other. Aasgard cleared his throat. "We need to stick to the plan. Light the torches!"

A soft glow illuminated the imposing forest before us. The wind whispered through the tree branches, sounding like a bag of bones being shaken. I took a moment to steel myself before we pushed onward. The shadows danced across the leaf-covered ground, playing games with my mind. *Was that noise an animal, or something worse?*

The trees swallowed us whole and the darker it got, the noisier it became. A shriek sounded off in the distance, making me pause briefly to search for it. We could only see the dancing shadows. "Keep going straight, nobody leave the path!" Aasgard growled.

I squinted as there appeared to be a structure emerging from the depth of the forest. A house possibly. Aasgard grinned. "There. The Hyroll's village!" But branches were cracking around us, and snake-like hisses rose from the bushes. We hurried into the safety of the village and spun around to face whatever was stalking us.

The darkness remained still, and for a moment I wondered if we had let the night play tricks on us. But then they finally appeared.

From the edges of the forest, twisted, horrid beings emerged. They walked on two legs with long talons digging into the soft earth underneath them. Long, snake-like tails flicked back and forth anxiously, as their beady eyes surveyed our army. Their hissing sounded like logs crackling on the fireplace. Thousands of these creatures towered over us with the heights of ogres. Claws flexed restlessly, dripping a clear substance that—while I was not completely certain what it was—could only spell out an agonizing death. "Why are we doing this again?" I whispered to Aasgard. He glared at me while every creature whipped their heads around to face me. *Their hearing must be phenomenal. Perfect.* Where was our hope of survival?

"We do this to live," Aasgard finally announced.

"And how do we plan on living against these things? I, for one, don't have a plan to defeat venomous demons," I snapped back.

He chuckled, the sound vibrating from deep within his chest. "That's simple. *We charge!*" His sword was brandished with a flourish, and the screams of war erupted around me in a deafening tone. Just like that, our army ran toward the enemy with seemingly suicidal thoughts drowning their tiny brains.

Our fight was for honor! For hope! For a lot of dumb reasons I couldn't wrap my head around. So I screamed, drew my own blade, and ran in the opposite direction.

Cottages blurred from my vision as I weaved around abandoned carts and stacks of hay to dodge the creatures leaping. Dear God, why could they leap after me? I was probably hyperventilating because one struck close enough to rip the back of my leather chest piece as if it were made of butter. The sword was practically useless as one creature crashed to my left and swiped high. I ducked with a high shriek, barely missing the long blades, and kept running with every ounce of strength I had.

More screams joined mine as the unmistakable sound of crushing bone and tearing flesh merged into the symphony of the night. I gagged while focusing on the buildings before me. A small barn caught my eye. The door was open and only a single torch burned inside. I could snuff it out and hide in the hay! My boots slid on the dirt as I attempted to stop mid-run to make a sharp left for safety. That slide saved my neck from being gouged by another creature. It also reminded me that I have been trained for combat and could probably take out a few of these guys myself.

Nyx-Ente let out a mighty bellow as he fell from the sky onto the creature's back. I hadn't the slightest clue where he'd come from, but I thanked the gods for his crazy appearance into my life. I flashed him a short wave of gratitude while I ran for the barn and left the battle in his experienced hands. It just made sense to leave.

The torch flickered, threatening to go out with the breeze as I finally neared my haven. I took the last step inside the door and tripped over a piece of broken cobblestone. I fell face first onto the dust-covered ground with an "oomph" and slid about two inches inside the barn. Not the entrance I was looking for, but I made it. I groaned and rubbed my chin, coughing as the dust drifted back down to the ground. It could have been so much worse. I might have slid farther and smashed my head into the barrels filling the small space. I blinked. Not a barn. A long storage place of sorts. I climbed to my feet, knees aching from the sudden impact, and took in the amazing number of barrels that someone had carefully stacked along the stone walls. At the end of the room was another door that appeared to be barely hanging on its hinges.

Curiosity got the best of me. With the dim light of the torch, I carefully opened a barrel and peered inside. Black sand. I popped up another barrel lid. More black sand. I blinked as someone crashed into the door. I whipped around with a yelp and came eye to eye with Aasgard. Good to see he was still breathing somehow. His bloodshot eyes stared at me in confusion before slowly taking in the barrels I had opened. "Boy." He breathed. "You are mad but brilliant! We shall sing of your courage once this night is done!"

What?

I opened my mouth to ask him what on Earth he was talking about, but the lumbering buffoon turned on his heels and started hollering out into the night! "Over here, ya giant worthless sacks of meat! Come and get your fill of *death*!"

For the second time today, I screamed in terror as Aasgard flapped his arms around and drew in the attention of the venomous demon horde, "Let's go!"

I spun on my heels and bolted for the opposing door. The rusted metal gleamed like a sweet beacon as a torch was shifted behind me. Three feet away the ground quaked under my feet. I stumbled but continued to propel myself forward as the unearthly shrieks of demons filled the corridor. I tucked my arms in close, and when the door came into range, I smashed into it with my left shoulder. The door gave way from the weight of my attack and clear night air kissed my cheeks. A dull throb had started in my shoulder, but I could care less. I was free! I was alive!

Still, I kept pressing forward until my lungs threatened to pop within my chest. I nearly made it back to the tree line, panting heavily as a shiver ran up my spine. Dark shadows shifted with the breeze. Maybe I should have run in a different direction. I turned as a thundering boom shook the ground, and a giant fireball lit up the sky. Hot flames swept out, consuming the buildings I had just passed in my mad dash towards safety. Sweat dotted my brow as the hellish fire continued its destructive path toward the forest in front of me. I swallowed hard and spun around again, despite my poor, protesting feet.

What on Pallam created that?

I ran again, dodging low hanging branches and wildly jumping over tree roots. Leaves crunched under my boots, and bushes snagged on my tunic, slowing me for a second before snapping and freeing me. Fire was lighting my way, which I was oddly thankful for. It was better than running blind, I supposed.

I didn't know how far I had made it. Sweat was pouring into my eyes, and though I tried to wipe it away, it was becoming harder to see. My clothes stuck to my body like a second skin, and muscles burned with every movement. The light was dimming. Perhaps it was safe. I kept running until my legs finally gave out.

Gasping for air, I lay down on the dried leaves and looked up at the sky. I was lost. I was in more pain than I had ever known before, and my eyes were too heavy to keep open. A branch snapped to the right of me as my vision started to close in on itself. *I'm so sorry, Gilbert,* I thought as my eyes fell shut. A soft voice floated to my ears, but it was muffled. Then there was nothing.

CHAPTER FOUR

THE SMELL OF herbs tickled my nose and slowly roused me from slumber. I stretched my arms up and rolled onto one side. That was a bad idea. Pain lanced through my body, and I jerked upright with a howl.

"Careful, those wounds haven't fully healed yet," a soft voice called from deeper in the cabin. *Cabin?* I rubbed my eyes and settled more comfortably on the small cot. "When did I get here?"

A soft chuckle rang out. "When I found you at dawn in the forest. Not a safe place for a traveler to be."

I was sitting inside a tiny room, only ten paces across. The bed was pushed against a wooden wall with a tiny rounded window that overlooked the forest outside. Sunshine filtered through a thick canopy of leaves. The effect was bright, beautiful even. Had I not experienced what I recently had, I would have merely sat back and let myself get lost in the serenity of nature. But nature tried to kill me, so forget that. *I'm going to be a kingdom boy. Only stone and metal surroundings from here on out.*

A door was situated directly by the foot of the bed, swinging outward to an equally small hallway. A locked chest stood at my bedside, where my leather vest and tunic—patched up from the branches that had snagged the soft fabric— were laid neatly across the top. I shifted the quilt away from my body and took stock of my surroundings. Bandages had been neatly placed across my ribs, one on top of my right arm and shoulder. A few smaller ones were obvious in seemingly random spots on my legs.

The night before had been rough, but had it really banged me up this badly? I swung my legs off the side of the bed and slowly stood up. When my aching legs were able to support my weight, I made my way out of the door and into the tiny hall. It only extended about seven steps and ended at a combination living/dining area, where a woman cloaked in grey from head to toe tended to a cauldron over a small fireplace. The scent of herbs radiated from whatever she was stirring.

Licking my dry lips, I quietly asked "May I have some water?"

Without even glancing up at me, the woman gestured to the round table with two place settings. I stepped carefully behind her and picked up the closest goblet. It was full, so I gulped the sweet juice inside.

After returning the goblet to the table empty, I felt a

warm and pleasant buzz settle in my stomach. "Wine?"

"My own brew," she confirmed. "When I found you and realized you were injured, I figured you would need something stronger than water when you awoke."

I tipped my head. "Thank you. May I ask who you are?"

The woman chuckled again and paused her stirring. "I am Isla of the forest, and you are?"

"Paul Paulson, the third of my name."

"Pleasure, Paul Paulson of the third descent, now tuck in to lunch, dear," Isla said as she ladled generous portions of soup into the two bowls. *How could I say no to that?* I smiled and settled into one of the small wooden chairs. It was surprisingly comfortable, and the food smelled amazing. My stomach growled before Isla was even fully seated, and I felt the heat rise up to my face. She waved it off and pointed to my bowl. "Eat."

A few moments passed while we filled our mouths with food. Isla was an amazing cook; the broth was rich in flavor, and I swore it soothed all my aching muscles.

She cleared her throat and finally broke the short silence. "So, Paul the third, tell me what brings you out into the Forest of Death?"

I nearly choked on my soup. "Forest of Death?"

The old woman threw her head back and cackled, revealing an ancient, weathered face. Her long silver hair had been tied back.

"That's what I'm callin' it," She paused, and a somber expression replaced her previously pleasant one. "Of course, it didn't use to be this way... But that's neither here nor there. Where are you going?"

I offered her a half shrug. "I was hoping to go home, but I guess the magic that keeps the barrier up needs to be broken first."

Isla raised a thin eyebrow at me. "Does it really? How did you get here?"

"Well, I kind of fell down the mountainside and landed here."

"Did you try leaving the same way you came in?"

I paused, the thought had never occurred to me. And now I felt stupid. I opened my mouth but closed it. Dammit. Of course, it didn't matter now. I couldn't leave Gilbert behind.

"Regardless, what was your plan to destroy the barrier?" she continued.

Fish out of water again. The plan sounded simple on paper, but I guessed I had never thought that through either. "Break into the castle. Smash the magic orb and then leave?" It sounded lame to my own ears, and from the frown on her face, she had the same thought.

"That easy?"

"I was hoping it would be."

She shook her head and stood. On her way into the tiny kitchen, she grabbed a jug and refilled my glass, along with her own. "Child, nothing is ever that easy around here."

My stomach sank with my hope. *Why?* So far, my entire adventure had been one crazy hard battle after another. Her revelation shouldn't be any surprise.

"You're tired. You aren't a fighter by birth, and this kingdom has tested you in ways you've never dreamed of before." Her words drifted across the room.

I raised a brow before taking another tentative drink of the wine. "Can you read minds?"

She laughed and settled back in her seat. "No, I've just seen enough to get really good at guessing. I wish I could say you didn't have to keep going anymore, but with how the situation has changed, there is no safe place to live nearby. You could go back up to the mountain, I suppose. However, I have a feeling that in doing so you'll be abandoning much more than just the chance to be a hero."

I glanced at the living room window and shivered. More of those demons could be lurking around too. I definitely didn't want to face them again, but she was right. I might be a coward, but my donkey depended on me. I couldn't let him down without even trying.

"Those creatures only emerge during the night time," Isla whispered.

I raised a brow. "You're sure you can't read minds?"

She cackled again. I may be a witch, but even I have limits, child."

A witch... That oddly made sense. I took a moment

to steel myself before finally braving the dreaded question. "I don't suppose you know the way to the castle from here?"

She grinned. "As a matter of fact, I do."

Before embarking on my journey, Isla drew me a bath with magic-infused water. It healed the rest of my wounds and gave me a perk of energy that lent an extra skip to my step. She also washed and dried—though I don't know how—my clothing so I was as fresh as I would be back home. It helped raise my spirits even though I was still leaving on what seemed like a weird suicide mission.

"Follow the blueberry bushes east. They will take you to the village outside this area. And be quick. You don't want to be caught during the night again. But keep your steps light. You could awaken the creatures by mistake," she warned while handing me a bag of apples and some rolls. "If you find yourself wounded and alone again, eat the bread. I've added a bit of magic to help you heal."

I stepped onto Isla's small worn pathway and paused and turned to face her. "I really don't know how to thank you for all of this."

She dismissed my gratitude with a slight wave of her hand and picked up a small wicker basket from beside the front door. "Think nothing of it. Now get going, I have herbs to pick, and I can't do that while entertaining you."

I raised an eyebrow at her, which made her cackle. "You didn't think magic came from thin air, did ya? I need some supplies to help me conjure my spells and keep the potions alive."

"I never thought about it before. But that makes sense… I think. Uh, did you want some help? It would be my way to repay you for all of your kindness to a needy stranger." I turned back around when she shrugged.

"What about your donkey?" she asked.

"He would understand me taking ten minutes out of my trip to help out an old woman," I said with a grin. Isla shook her head but headed toward a group of tall plants near her small cottage.

"You're an odd one, Paul Paulson the third, but very well. Just don't get left behind. I'm a very busy old lady, thank you." She glanced at me over her shoulder and winked.

CHAPTER FIVE

I SPENT EVEN more than the expected ten minutes picking plants with Isla, but it was easy to get lost in the repetitive nature of the task. Some of the plants were tiny, white flowers, some were long vines that grew nearly as big as I was, and others looked like regular weeds. Through it all, she kept the conversation light until almost two hours had passed, and then she shooed me away.

"You need to go before the sun sets. Don't want to find yourself in that situation again," she reminded me as she gently took the full basket from my hands.

"What about you? Aren't you afraid of those things since you live here?"

She chuckled and shook her head. "I'm made of magic, dear boy. Most creatures will leave me alone if I will it to be. But my magic only stretches so far. Once you're off my property, the protection spell will be gone and you will face the dangers this world holds."

I nodded quietly and rubbed the back of my neck. I wasn't exactly thrilled about this journey, but the peace had to end at some point. Reality could only be stalled for so long. Again, she patted my shoulder and gave me a warm smile. "You're a lot stronger than you realize. It'll be difficult, but I know you'll do just fine."

With that, I started back toward the path of blueberry bushes. *I wish I felt the confidence she had in me. I don't know what kind of strength a man who ran from violence could have, but I would certainly use it differently if it truly did exist. Would I really?* I paused for a moment and looked up at the sky. I'd like to think that if I had any strength, I would be like Aasgard, running into battle with my sword held up high. I would take on my enemies without any hesitation to rid the world of evil and injustice. If I had any strength, I would be the hero they all thought I was.

But I didn't have any, so I wasn't. That was a depressing thought. But, the thought occurred to me, maybe a hero didn't need to be the swiftest guy on the field. Maybe being a hero meant something more. I chewed on my bottom lip while I pondered that further. Maybe I could help everyone by doing something I actually knew how to do...

I groaned, yeah right... How could I help an army with my fantastic ability to craft fine pans? Or sell them for a reasonable price? Hell, being honest with myself, I had to admit that I didn't even have a plan to rescue Gilbert. If I couldn't fend anything off, how was I supposed to get him out of the clutches of evil winged demons?

I was so immersed in my own thoughts that I didn't see him until he grabbed me from behind. Arms of steel wrapped around my chest and lifted me clean off my feet. It felt as though my back was pressed against a stone wall. I reacted on instinct and screamed while flailing my legs around, connecting with the man's legs occasionally. The man grunted, "Easy there, killer. Was just sayin' hi."

Relief flooded my entire body. "Nyx-Ente?"

"Hello there, mighty hero. How on earth did ya make it this far without us seein' ya?" I was promptly dropped onto my feet and spun around to face his wide, toothy grin.

I shook my head in disbelief. "It's a long story."

"Well, are ya still comin'?"

I grinned up at him. "Yeah, I'm still with you all. Let's go break a barrier and stop an evil king!"

He bellowed and slapped me on the back, making me stumble forward a few steps before I managed to regain my balance. "That's the spirit! To war!"

But keep your steps light, you don't want to awaken any creatures by mistake.

The witch's warning whispered through my mind as I watched Nyx-Ente walk back toward the group. I had a difficult time swallowing while darting quick glances at the area around us. Nothing but a few small birds calling out to one another in the distance. No weird shadows moving. No sounds of branches cracking save for what my large friend stepped on. Perhaps the witch had been overly cautious.

Nyx-Ente paused when he realized I was still rooted to my spot. He raised an eyebrow at me and waved his hand. "I thought ye were comin'? What's gotcha lost in thought?"

The ground vibrated underneath my boots. My eyes grew wide as I looked down then back up at Nyx-Ente. His brows were scrunched together in confusion as he probably felt the same thing. "Uh-oh," was all I managed to say before the ground between us exploded.

Long tree roots came to life before our eyes and reached up for the bright sky. I involuntarily took a step back and shielded myself from the falling dirt and leaves. The roots, possibly ten in total, paused for a moment. Then they split up and attacked. Five long arms snapped down at me with tiny thorns adorning their massive length. I screamed as I turned on my heel and ran from the assault.

Their reach appeared endless! I jumped and crashed through bushes and over fallen branches. Still, the pursuit continued no matter how much ground I put between myself and the origins of their arrival. Then, five more appeared with small bursts within the ground, mere feet away from my left side. I ducked underneath a branch as it lashed out at my head, and I nearly fell to my knees as I tried to push forward. *The witch,* I thought as I jumped over a low strike. *I need to make it back to the witch. She's lived here for years. Surely, she knows how to force these atrocities back to where they came.*

I heard a bellow behind me and dared a quick look back. Nyx-Ente had tried to follow me, but the roots had snagged him. They wound around his stomach and chest, pulling him back into the depth of the forest. Blood was seeping from his injuries, and I knew the expression of anguish etched upon his face would forever be branded in my memory. That one moment of looking back sealed my own fate. A root had emerged from the ground in front of me, and I didn't see it in time to jump. The long, thick tentacle wrapped around my ankle, halfway up my calf, and yanked me to the ground with it.

Pain shot up through my body as the tiny thorns dug into my flesh like miniature teeth. My pursuer jerked again and yanked me back with my friend. The ground was hard and unforgiving on my torso, but I ignored it long enough to reach into my belt and unsheathe a small knife. My knuckles had turned white as I gripped it with all my strength. I reached down to cut myself free. The root was tough, and my blade scored the bark, but it didn't slice through as I had hoped. I held myself awkwardly up to saw slowly through the limb and cringed each time my bottom smacked over a rock as we propelled toward its home.

Whatever the thing was that held us captive didn't seem to like my attempts to get free. About a quarter of the way through the root, others joined their comrade in seizing my arms and waist. I struggled against the tight hold, grinding my teeth as the thorns dug further into my bared wrists and tore through my clothing. Agony threatened to steal my consciousness again but the closer we came to the gaping hole in the ground, the more I gained strength. In the end, my struggle was to no avail. Nyx-Ente cried out for help as his body was dragged underground. Shortly after his descent, I followed him downward into the large cavern of clay and rock. The area was almost a perfect cylinder with enough space to drag two large males down at a time and still have room to spare. The roots wrapped themselves tighter around my body as they lowered me into the world below. The sunlight dimmed above us, before shrinking and then disappearing as the cavern took a sudden turn left turn and dropped into an imposing underground cave.

The beast we had angered finally came into sight. Partly submerged in a pool of water on the floor, its entire form seemed to be made of bark with a wide onion-shaped body. I couldn't figure out if the creature had any eyes or a mouth, but roots sprouted mostly from the top of its body. Our captor had hundreds of them.

I gawked at the creature who was partly submerged in a pool of water on the cavern's floor. The room spanned at least one hundred yards long and, from what I could see, was dimly lit by glowing fungus on the walls and ceiling. Water trickled in from tiny cracks in the foundation. Oddly enough, I recalled a story about finding an escape from a cave by following the sounds of water. But down in this lair, we appeared to be surrounded by it.

The creature pulled us closer before unceremoniously dropping each of us into the pool. I quickly learned two things from the five-foot drop. One, the water was only knee high. And two, what appeared as water actually wasn't.

Nyx-Ente had somehow managed to land on his feet while I dropped onto hands and knees. The impact with the hard bottom stung and jarred my bones, but the liquid I was in burned worse than anything I had ever felt. I quickly raised my hands out, one still curled around the hilt of my knife. I'd never seen skin such a bright pink color even with sunburn. A moment later, the situation registered that we needed to get onto dry land as quickly as possible. I stood up and was horrified to see my pant legs evaporate into thin air.

"This thing doesn't need a mouth to chew. It secretes a stomach acid-like liquid, then draws the nutrients left behind back in through its roots." Nyx-Ente said.

Already my legs were turning red from the acid, and my blood was running freely into the pond. The roots in question wrapped back around us, shaking the ground and splashing that horrid goo up in the process.

"Head for the walls and climb! Get yerself out of this acid!" Nyx-Ente roared as he drew a broadsword from the sheath on his back. I slipped my knife back into its sheath, shielded my face and sprinted like a madman for safety. The roots ignored my movement as if they knew I had no real chance of escaping. That realization was depressing and exhilarating. At least I wouldn't have to fight my way to safety, even if it only lasted five minutes because I'd never climbed a stone wall before.

"What are you doing?" I called out as I reached for a large rock protruding from the water.

"Kill the roots. Kill the plant. I'm gonna send this thing to hell!"

I scrambled up the slick surface of the stone and darted a quick glance behind me. "What? Are you insane?"

"Nah, I want to live, and this is how ya do it," Nyx-Ente answered. His tone as firm as he slashed at the nearest feasting root. The blade cut cleanly through the creature, but the attack riled up the rest of the roots surrounding him. They drew out of the acid and poised to strike back. I couldn't watch it. Nyx-Ente's legs were bleeding at a steady pace as he lingered in the pool, and I noticed the shadows of fatigue under his eyes. None of our actions were going to work. He couldn't last long enough to cut down the hundreds of roots this massive beast had grown. But Nyx-Ente's actions might keep the creature distracted long enough for me to climb back up the hole we'd come through.

I swallowed down the guilt that came with the thought. No, I couldn't leave the poor guy behind. I bit my bottom lip and surveyed the area once more. There had to be a way to defeat this damned thing, so we could both live to see tomorrow. I squinted at the odd onion-shaped body. The monster was almost perfectly rounded. *What was keeping it standing straight up?* Especially with the weight of the tentacles sprouted from the top of its head…

This thing appeared like a bowl with a flat bottom I couldn't see from my vantage point. Or, it had more roots keeping it anchored in the ground. Nobody ever called me a genius, but I was willing to bet the roots sprouting from the top weren't roots at all but rather branches, like tree tops. Inside the pool of acid was the real root system that kept this thing anchored and safe. If I was wrong, we would die. If I was right, we still could die because this beast was no joke.

I took a deep breath, withdrew my short sword, and jumped back into the acid. While the branch tentacles were distracted with Nyx-Ente, I dove straight for the body of the beast. It was perfectly curved, so to reach underneath it I would have to submerge more of my body into the acid. The burning pain was already enough to slow me down. I was terrified that any more and I would be lost to the agony of flesh dissolving from my bones. I caught a glimpse of the fight my friend was engaged in and watched as a branch wrapped around his right arm and slammed him against the cave wall. His body made a sickening cracking sound as it crashed into the unforgiving surface and then dropped lifelessly back into the pool.

I had no other choice. I needed to swallow back as much as I could and end this damned thing.

Just two feet away from the beast's body, I dropped to my knees and slid the rest of the way to its massive form. Thankfully, I was right. Underneath, barely visible even up close, was a series of smaller roots anchoring the body to the pool's bottom. I gripped my sword with both hands, thrust it underneath the creature, and started to pull to the right. I heard a soft snap and threw more of my body into the attack. My belly, half of my chest and part of my shoulder were fully submerged in the acid. The rancid smell was nauseating, and the burning felt as though it was consuming my entire being.

I bit my bottom lip and pulled harder. A branch wrapped itself around my chest, the tiny thorns digging into the leather that was weakening with each second and starting to pull me back. I gasped and released one hand from the hilt of my blade. Soon, my free fingers found a small root and wrapped around it. I adjusted the blade's angle to start slicing toward my own body. Dumb. Dangerous. Didn't really matter at that point.

The more the branch yanked against my body, the more damage I did to the roots. Snap, snap, snap… One by one they were slowly giving away. Tears rolled down my face as I locked my jaw and kept the blade snagged under as many of the anchors as possible. I wanted to scream. I wanted to give up. I just wanted it to end!

I was so lost in my own thoughts that I hadn't noticed the rounded body tipping on its side. Without roots to anchor it, the thing was beginning to roll over. A branch snapped down on my back like a whip, and I screamed as I felt skin slice open and the wound fill up with acid. My eyes blinked, and my vision was out of focus. I couldn't stop. I couldn't give up.

I had forgotten what I was doing or why it was important. Thoughts were whittled down to basic words and raw feeling. Crack. The branch snapped down on my back again. I had to… Had to… I needed to keep… Something. I had to do… Something.

I groaned as my body sank farther and farther into the pool. Crack. I couldn't feel my own body anymore. I saw the fuzzy outline of the blade in my hand, but my fingers were too numb to hold it. Crack. How was I still hanging onto it? Nyx-Ente screamed in the distance. Crack. Blinking again, I slowly opened my eyes to see that I was almost five feet away from the man-eating onion.

"Hold on, jus' hold on. We're getting out of here. Yer okay. Hold on." I tried to look up at Nyx-Ente but couldn't get my head to cooperate. It just lolled to the side. I opened my mouth and tasted salty tears. *Was I crying? Why? What was going on?*

"Yer one hell of a hero. Now, keep that head up. We gotta get back to yer donkey, remember? Stay with me, Paul." I tried to say something back, but words came out as a gargle instead. "Rrrooogs. Meed da rrroolllls." I was cold and tired. So, for the second time since the adventure started, I passed out. And everything ended just as I'd prayed it would.

CHAPTER SIX

I WAS STARING down at my delicious soup before I realized Isla was talking to me with a faint smile on her lips. "What?"

"Did you try leaving the same way you came in?" That seemed like a ridiculous question. A barrier prevented anyone from leaving. *Didn't she remember that?*

"No. I can't," I stated flatly while pushing my spoon around in the bowl of soup. Suddenly, I wasn't very hungry anymore.

"How did you get here?" She continued to push the topic, which was getting on my nerves. *Didn't we have this conversation before?*

"Well, I kind of fell down the mountainside and landed here."

"What was your plan to destroy the barrier?" She asked as she rose from her seat.

Sunlight filtered in through the treetops. It cast a

soft, golden glow on the land. "Break into the castle. Find Gilbert. Smash the magic orb, and then leave." It still sounded lame to my own ears. From the expression on her face, she had the same thought.

"That easy?"

"I was hoping it would be that easy."

Isla shook her head and stood, making her way into the tiny kitchen and grabbing a jug. When she brought it back, Isla refilled my glass and then her own. "Child, nothing is ever that easy around here."

I flashed her a crooked smile. "In general, nothing ever is."

She carefully set the jug down on the table and chuckled. "Really? Aren't you a pots and pans creator? And salesman? Are you telling me that is difficult?"

I sipped my drink and nodded yet refused to meet her eyes, "If I'm being honest with myself, then yeah. It was hard to learn how to make pots and pans. It can be extremely hard to sell them. Most days I barely break even. It might not be as difficult as taking down a patriarchy, but that doesn't make it easy either."

She nodded thoughtfully in return and took a delicate sip of her own soup. "So why are you doing it?"

I groaned and leaned back in my chair. For some odd reason, it hurt. Especially my left shoulder. It felt as if I had a horrible sunburn. Or like someone took a cheese grater to my skin. *The explosion couldn't have been that bad, could it?*

"Why are you asking me this?"

Isla cocked her head to the side and shrugged. "Why do you keep asking yourself the same things? I figured you would have an answer by now. I'm just a curious old bat, I suppose."

Wait a second here…

I narrowed my gaze at her. We'd had this conversation before. Or, sort of. A few new questions had been asked but it was pretty much the same. I wasn't recently in an explosion. Shit! I was being eaten by some weird type of plant! Kind of suspicious that I'd practically just left her house and was already dreaming about her… I sat up straight and opened my mouth to voice one of the thousands of questions in my mind, but Isla simply waved goodbye at me, and everything went black again.

***

Sudenly, I jolted awake, panting heavily as if I'd been chased. Probably had been, but surely that adventure had ended quite some time ago. A woman I'd never seen before rushed to my side with her hands held up in concern. Her long, green robes swished as she approached. "Careful! Your wounds are still healing. You shouldn't move so suddenly." She paused and offered me a heartwarming smile. "You're safe now, you know."

I blinked at her in confusion and gradually took stock of my surroundings. The narrow bed where I lay was in a small, patchwork tent. Bandages covered me from my navel up to my neck and wrapped around both arms down to the tips of my fingers. I must have resembled a mummy. A thin, scratchy blanket covered my lap, which I was grateful for. I wasn't sure I wanted to see what kind of damage had been done down below. However, despite outward appearances, I felt absolutely fine. My left shoulder was a bit sore perhaps, but I certainly didn't feel as bad as Isla had clearly expected me to be.

I stared up at the woman again and took in her heart-shaped face with a soft glow on rosy cheeks. Her chestnut hair was twisted into a loose bun at the right side of her head and held together with ribbons and decorative sticks. Those big, bright green eyes took care in regarding me back.

"I'm sorry," I mumbled, "but who are you?"

She blushed, and her plump, pink lips turned into a small O. "I'm so sorry, sir, I'm Jez'ra, one of the healers here."

I nodded. "It's a pleasure, Jez'ra. I'm Paul Paulson the third. Unfortunately, I don't have time to lie around in bed all day—I have things to do, and quickly." I slung my legs around to the edge of the cot and carefully stood up. While I still had pants on, I could see portions of white peeking out from the bottoms. Again, the woman fussed and attempted to coax me back into the bed, but I remained firm and stepped forward. She backed up with a sharp gasp and looked around frantically.

"I honestly have no idea how you are standing right now. I tended to your wounds myself. They were horrible and so extensive! You must listen to me. Pushing yourself will only make things worse for you later on!"

I shrugged. "Probably, but honestly, I feel fine. See?"

I found an edge to the bandages around my left right and tugged to unwind it back to the middle of my arm. Pale, but flawless, if I do say so myself, flesh without so much as a papercut was revealed.

Jez'ra gasped and took a step closer to inspect my arm as if it were a foreign creature. "That… That isn't possible. It's only been a few hours since…" she trailed off as she marveled over the mysterious implications left unspoken.

"Really? Only a few hours?" I asked as I continued to pull myself free from the white strips of cloth. "That's fantastic! There's still time to save Gilbert!"

"Excuse me, but who is Gilbert?"

I started for the door but flashed her a quick smile as I brushed past. "He's my donkey."

The poor girl looked as though she had never been so confused in her entire life. Regardless, I needed to check on Nyx-Ente and then get back on track. The days were ticking away, and the more time I spent

54

galivanting around in the woods, the more time Gilbert was at risk of being devoured.

I ducked out of the tent and ran straight into Aasgard's broad chest. When I stumbled back and looked up at his hardened face, disapproval was radiating off him in thick waves. I offered a guilty, uncertain smile and tiny hand wave. "Hey there, so uh… how is everything?"

Could I have been any more awkward?

Aasgard regarded me for a moment in silence. The seconds that passed seemed like hours as I swallowed thickly and shifted on my feet.

"I've seen many things over the years. But never have I witnessed someone heal so quickly from such burns," he said while stroking his beard.

I didn't have an answer for him since I didn't understand it myself. "What about Nyx-Ente?"

"Healed, though not as well as you, and ready to go raise hell." Aasgard chuckled. I smiled and scratched the back of my neck. "Yeah, that sounds like him. How about everyone else? What happened when we were separated?"

Aasgard's face fell with a soft sigh. He stepped to the side and let me see the extent of our small camp. We were on the outside of the forest, though mere feet away from the tree line. Only five tents had been erected, and one small bonfire was burning in the middle of the scattered circle. Men and women who walked about wore stony expressions and exhibited new scars. Dirt, mud, and leaves stuck to their armor and in their hair. Since we'd entered the forest and encountered the first horde of demons, our numbers had been cut nearly in half.

Aasgard explained that I wasn't the only member who'd been separated from the group, but I was the only one found. Even after they'd heard mine and Nyx-Ente's cries for help when the branches of the plant monster arose, they fanned out to keep the search going. But now that it was early evening, the search parties had been called back. We couldn't afford to spend more hours searching for the others. It was time to start moving forward again

My heart broke for the fallen, but it only filled me with more determination to help the remaining warriors however I could. Everyone in the group was battered but ready to see this journey finally end.

"Remember, the village should be only a mile and a half away from Hyroll's Forest. We will go around it quietly but swiftly. Don't start any fights with the villagers. Keep your mind on the plan," Aasgard announced.

Everyone nodded and proceeded forward. But once we crossed over a small hill outside the village, we saw only a massive burnt circle in its place. Nothing remained except for a single broken cart wheel, at the edge of the former town. We all stopped to stare in confusion and growing horror. "How did this happen?"

someone cried from behind me.

"Firebomb. And a mighty big one from the looks of it," a gravelly voice replied.

"But… Why?" I whispered.

The young man next to me shook his head in sadness. "He doesn't need a reason to do the things he does."

I felt nauseous as we skirted the charred remains of the village. It was difficult to think about what'd happened here. *Had the village been evacuated before the attack landed?* I wanted to believe so, but I knew deep down that wasn't true. *What was the point of wiping out an empty town?* There wasn't one. Then again, I didn't see the point in mass murder either. *Who could create such a threat that the king needed to kill every innocent soul?*

"Watch yer step. There could still be traps lying underneath the grass," Nyx-Ente warned with a solemn glance at me. I nodded. Nowhere is completely safe until the negative magic affecting this kingdom was reversed. I had learned that lesson the hard way. Technically, I got it from the witch, but who could have imagined a man-eating plant hidden away in a secret underground cave?

"Maybe we should fan out. If someone gets caught in something nasty, we'll need free members to help them escape," I suggested. When everyone stopped and stared at me, I felt extremely uncomfortable. "What?"

"Brilliant idea, hero. We'll fan out and keep a close eye on one another. At the first sign of trouble, alert the others so we can jump in before the situation gets too out of hand," Aasgard announced. The group nodded in unison, and we all moved into a large rectangle-like formation with approximately six feet between each warrior.

Watching everyone creep forward like inexperienced ninjas would have been funny if not for the severity of the situation. Even I had my arms out to steady myself and was toeing the grass before placing each foot firmly in front of the other. Aasgard carried a blade in hand with his eyes constantly sweeping over the terrain. The progress forward was slow moving, but we had no clue where the attack—if any—would come from. I swallowed hard and wiped at some sweat beading on my forehead. The whole scenario was too tense. Maybe nothing would happen. *Who would honestly booby-trap a desecrated village?* There wasn't any point to it.

Never question the mind of an evil king. They will never make sense.

CHAPTER SEVEN

AN OLDER MAN in the group took up the west side near the back of the trail. He stepped forward and in an instant, a small explosion ripped upward from the ground and consumed his body. He screamed as the flames tore through his clothing and ate away at his skin.

"Firebombs! Nobody move," Aasgard roared.

Several cries of sorrow echoed through the air until another small explosion went off. Then another. The group broke apart and started running in different directions. Some moved toward the ash that had been the village, thinking the burnt grounds couldn't maintain any buried secrets, while others rushed for the surrounding hills hoping the height would provide them some safety.

I stood paralyzed to my spot as I watched three warriors fall to their knees, shrouded in flames. The Dexlock twins were pouring their canteens of water over one of the bodies, but it was too late. The rapid, widespread destruction was beyond my comprehension. Aasgard shouted out more orders, but his words fell upon deaf ears. Nyx-Ente had his hands full of large rocks and was throwing them out into the distance. I blinked. *Why in heaven's name was he doing that? What exactly did he think he was going to accomplish?* Fighting fire with rocks was insane!

One of the stones landed with a heavy thump, and another firebomb exploded beneath it to contradict my thought. I felt stupid, but that wasn't unusual. The smell of burning flesh was giving me a headache, and it felt as if the heat was searing my own face. I gagged but bent down and started picking up anything I could find with weight. A small glass eye stared blankly up at me. I hesitated, but with a cringe, I added it to my arsenal.

Boom.

Boom.

Boom.

The thundering sounds shook the ground as hidden bombs detonated left and right. I threw one of the rocks down a mere foot in front of me, and when nothing happened, I stepped forward. Throw a rock. Move again. I repeated the action over and over. As long as I kept my mind off the chaos around me, I could keep pressing toward the goal. I threw another stone and was kicked back by the force of the explosion. My face burned from the heat… felt singed, and I thought my hair was smoking. I patted out the small sparks trying to ignite on my vest. My heart was racing, and it took two attempts before I could climb back to my feet.

The smaller rocks I had collected had dropped and scattered when I fell back from the blast, but I found a few of them to use while I inched away from the flames. That was when I realized our problem was growing. Every bomb that went off created a small fire that was slowly eating away at the dry grass beneath our feet. The resulting heat continued to set off more explosives hidden away around the village. Despite the rock trick, we were going to burn to death unless another plan could be formed.

So, what could I do? Run and die by explosion, or stand there and die by the rising flames? The heat was making me sweat. I bit my bottom lip, weighed the pros and cons, and then took off running with a girlish scream of terror.

Boom.

Boom.

Boom.

I almost lost my footing as the ground continued to explode all around me. Three feet from my left, another blast went off. Keeping my arms close to my body, I gritted my teeth and pushed at a pace faster than I thought possible. Aldron was to my right, running as he looked back in horror. "Don't look back! Stay focused on everything ahead!" I screamed.

He snapped his head straight, and together we weaved around pillars of flames and jumped over obstacles in our path. The ground was uneven, making the escape more difficult. My foot got caught in a rabbit hole, and I cried out as I pitched forward. Before my face smashed into the ground, a hand wrapped around my arm and tugged me back to my feet. I gave a relieved nod and sigh to Aasgard as he made sure I was steady before racing toward the opposite end of the village. I stayed behind him, my legs protesting with every lunge.

I vowed to myself that if I lived through the entire ordeal, I was never running again. Ever. I gulped and kept my eyes locked on the edges of the burnt circle. Only a few more feet and we would be safe. Or at least, I assumed we would be safe. The raging fire behind us was probably still going to be a problem, but I was most worried about losing my own feet.

Symol—or was that Jorgon— rapidly approached on my left. An explosion blasted next to him, but he twisted his body to narrowly avoid the worst of it. The momentum of the blast flung him forward, but the sly elf tucked in on himself and rolled, then sprung back up to his feet as if the threat was nothing more than an annoyance. What I wouldn't have given to be as composed as him.

Finally, I passed the last of the blackened ground

and was running through an open field. The ground started to incline, but I didn't stop until I was at the top of the hill. Panting heavily, I glanced back to see a few more stragglers making their way up behind me. Nyx-Ente was winded but appeared fine otherwise. *Thank the heavens.*

The fire was out of control—sweeping away the perfect circle that had once resembled a fallen village—turning the rest of the land into a desolate wasteland. I pulled the waterskin off my belt with trembling hands and took a greedy gulp before passing it to another warrior who looked ready to keel over. The man flashed me a grateful smile and drank deeply before passing the bag off again.

Aldron brushed some soot off his shoulder and turned to our leader. "So, that was what destroyed the village?"

Aasgard nodded and surveyed our smaller group. Only eighteen of the original forty remained. The odds were stacked against us. "Firebombs are magically infused creations that detonate upon impact. All it took was our feet pressing on the tops of their containers, for example. A typical firebomb is only the size of a dinner plate, maybe a foot wide, and usually compacted into a thin square to resemble a tile. It's a nasty trap, but I imagine the one that destroyed this village was at least the size of the castle base. That, or they dropped several smaller ones in quick succession to blow up the villagers before anyone had time to escape."

"So," Aldron continued, "it's safe to say the king has more at his castle."

Aasgard nodded, his face grave as he took one last glimpse at the roaring flames before turning away. "And much worse."

I rubbed a hand down my face. "Are we still sticking with the original plan then? Storm in and magically find this orb to destroy it before the guards kill everyone in the castle?"

Aasgard sighed. "We don't have any other choice. If we don't take out the king, our situation will only get worse. Yes, we may die in the process, but if we don't try, hundreds will surely perish in the king's conquest."

My headache was getting worse. I followed the group as they crept down the side of the hill, away from the fire but straight toward the gates of hell. My heart was heavy, and hope was all but lost. I doubted we could make it to the gates, much less get inside. For a moment I wondered if Gilbert was still alive. For the thousandth time, I mulled over the worth of the trek itself. *If I made it to the highest tower and found the bones of my friend inside, could I really turn around and continue with this path? Would dying be worth it if he were never saved?*

I watched the men and women still standing and making forward progress. Each one of them bore similar expressions. We were all beginning to doubt that our noble cause would change anything. Our goal was seemingly impossible. Maybe we'd survived the worst of our encounters, but our luck wouldn't last forever. The reality was standing in front of us, and it was cold and bleak. *What kept us moving? We were all marching toward our deaths with weapons ready to be drawn?*

Something squeaked beneath my foot, I lowered my head and saw a small, tattered doll. I stopped and picked it up. A woman near me paused and searched her pockets before spinning around with wide, frightened eyes. When she noticed the toy in my hands, relief was written all over her face. I approached her and handed the doll over. She accepted it with a muttered, "Thank you," before lovingly tucking it away again in the pocket of her robes.

The journey wasn't about any of us. It was about our loved ones. That was why we kept walking, even though it might be to our own demise.

CHAPTER EIGHT

THE GROUP CONTINUED for another mile or so south until it became too dark to keep going. We set up a small camp and started the bonfire. Nyx-Ente took a few members with him to hunt for fresh meat while I helped chop some herbs for dinner. Thankfully, a stream was close by to refresh our water supply and fill the cauldron for a stew.

I would have suggested fishing, but the stream was so small that any of the guppies inside wouldn't be big enough to provide us with enough nourishment. Besides, I didn't know how to fish.

Once dinner was cooked and dished out, we tucked in with only stilted conversation breaking the silence. Everyone avoided the topic of war, or what had happened to us previously. Instead, we exchanged stories about the lives we'd once lived… the hobbies once enjoyed, and the cherished memories that each of us kept close to our heart.

"When I was younger, I was afraid of thunderstorms. Every time a storm arrived in town, and my parents were away working, I would run to the stables and hide with Gilbert. Except he wasn't any braver than me and would curl up on my lap and cry. Do you know how loud donkeys can be? They can get really loud! So here I was, just a boy with a donkey as big as myself with his head on my lap crying until the storm passed. I thought I was going to be deaf before I reached adulthood." I chuckled. "When I got older, I outgrew the fear, but Gilbert never did. When I stopped going to the stables, he would break out and sneak into our house to climb into my bed with me. I had no clue how he did it. I changed the locks to the stable doors many times, but the stubborn old mule would still find his way into my room. Once he broke my window doing so!"

Everyone around the campfire watched in anticipation of more stories.

"So, I stopped keeping him out and gave up on owning a bed. I moved the mattress to the floor since he weighed so much that he would break the wooden frame, and just slept where he could find me any time he was scared. To this day, I still pay the local oracle to check for storms before traveling, so I can avoid them."

Jorgon/Symol shook his head with a grin. "Why do you go through such troubles for such a crazy creature?" he asked.

I shrugged and picked at the bark on the log where

I was sitting. "We grew up together and have been through a lot but always side by side. He might seem like just a donkey to everyone else, but to me, he's my best friend. Heck, he's my only friend, if I'm being honest." I paused with a small frown. "I guess that sounds kind of pathetic."

"Nothin' pathetic about friendship. It doesn't matter if yer friend is human or beast. Loyalty is somethin' to take pride in," Nyx-Ente declared.

My face heated and I mumbled, "Yeah I suppose."

"I think it is rather sweet," Jez'ra added. "I had a puppy growing up, and I loved him dearly. He passed away three years ago from old age, but I understand what you mean. He was my best friend, and I was so sad when he had to go. But he left me a gift—new friends to love and make new memories with."

I looked at her quizzingly. "How did he do that?"

"Well, after my village was attacked for not paying the proper taxes, I fled and ran into the mountains. It was pure luck that I met Aasgard there, who took me in. That was my dog's name, so I knew he had to have a hand, or paw, in our meeting! I became close to everyone while we ran from the evils of our world and worked together to figure out how to take the land back. I consider everyone here my friend. Even you, Sir Paul," she stated with a bright smile.

I blushed deeper and let out a soft laugh. "Uh, thanks. I consider you a friend too."

"And now Gilbert isn't your only friend." She giggled.

"Aye, we may be an army now, but I donna see you all as warriors. I see ye all as friends too," Nyx-Ente added.

"I as well. Friendship is important, especially in such dark times. Never take it for granted, and never let it go. Tomorrow, we're going to save your Gilbert and the rest of our friends in this kingdom. Tomorrow we will take down the king!" Aasgard nodded and raised his goblet high. The silver reflected flames of the bonfire and everyone's face who was sitting around it.

Aldron jumped up and held his own goblet in the air. "Here. Here."

"Here. Here!" we all joined in. The chorus of laughter sprang up and filled the lonely nighttime sky. I leaned back and looked at the stars. A huge smile crossed my mouth as others started telling stories about their friends over the years. I knew Gilbert was still alive. And I was going to bring him, and all my other friends, home

***

"What was your plan to destroy the barrier?" Isla asked.

I grinned at her and sat back in the comfortable wooden chair, decorated with plush cushions I was sure she'd sewn herself. "Break into the castle, find Gilbert, smash the magic orb, and then save my friends."

"That easy?"

"Of course, it won't be easy, but it's what I'm going to do regardless."

She stood to fetch the jug and refill our cups. Once they were topped off, she set the pitcher back on the table and settled into her own seat with a thoughtful nod. After taking a delicate sip of her soup, she asked, "So why are you doing it?"

"Because they're my best friends. And when you love someone, or something—like this kingdom—you fight for it. Even if you're afraid and tired, even if it isn't easy, you give it everything you have." I took a sip of soup.

"You're not a warrior," she said while eyeing me carefully. I stared into her unwavering gaze. "That's true."

"You've come a long way since you started your journey up the Forbidden Mountain, Paul Paulson the third."

I laughed. "It's funny what falling on an ogre will do to you."

She chuckled and stirred the contents in her bowl. "That's true. Fate works in mysterious ways. Now let me ask you this: Are you the hero from the prophecy?"

I leaned forward in the chair. "Here's my question to you. Does anyone know if they're a hero until the moment comes when it's time to do something heroic?

I can't say if I am or not, but I don't think anyone is just brought up knowing their own destiny either. So, I guess if it's in the cards… then I am. If it's not… I'm not."

"It is said that only the hero can defeat the evil that holds our lands. You would still do this even though you may die?"

"I've got to try to save my friends. Like I already said, love is worth fighting for, even if the odds are stacked against you. Besides, sometimes you don't need a hero to swoop in and save the day. I think that sometimes you just need that hope to see the light at the end of the tunnel. And once you've seen it, you know you'll have the strength to grab it."

"You certainly have the strength, Paul."

I stood and pushed my seat in. "Do you have any more questions, Isla of the Forest?"

She grinned with a twinkle in her eye. "Do you?" she shot back.

I returned her smile with a shake of my head. "Nope. I'm good."

"Then go out there and save your friends."

CHAPTER NINE

WE HID ON top of a hill overlooking the castle, staring at the skies for the signal that our second group had made it into position. After an hour of being crouched down, I began to fear that something horrible had happened to them. The castle stood tall and proud, with a stone gate around the outer perimeter. I don't know what I was expecting, but it wasn't the monstrosity that stood before us. The castle itself was as large as a small village. There could easily be hundreds of rooms inside, and without any details about the layout, we could spend hours searching for the king without getting anywhere. The gate doors were made of wood, and only four guards patrolled the outside. Getting in was going to be easier than I had anticipated. I looked up at four towers protruding from the castle's roof. Large figures circled and disappeared somewhere within them. At least I had somewhere to start. If I wanted to find Gilbert, then I needed to head upwards until I found the towers. Finally, a thin trail of smoke curled into the sky behind the castle.

"I hope you're already because this is it. No matter what happens, I want you to know that it's been an honor to fight alongside you all. You're fine men and women. Your legacy shall live on! Let's take back our kingdom!" Aasgard announced, drawing his blade from its sheath. We roared in agreement and rushed forward with our blades held high.

The guards were startled by our sudden rampage, yet they still drew their own blades and cried out to the others behind the gate. A loud BOOM shook the area with a plume of smoke that rose from behind the castle. We made quick work of the guards and then charged the gate. It must not have been locked- what kind of morons didn't gate the front gate? - because it slowly swung open from our combined weight. Inside the guards were scrambling. Their shouts were deafening, with a chorus of metal clashing against metal. They had better armor. They had demons patrolling the skies. We had every reason to win. The war was on.

I rushed towards the castle's front doors. I figured if I could make it inside, I had a better chance of surviving the chaos that had ensued. I needed to find and save Gilbert, then I would see if I could make it to the king on my own. It occurred to me that I would be taking a life today. I didn't think too hard about it but as I nearly tripped over a severed arm, I was forced to suddenly face the fact that blood would be spilt by my hands. Could I do it? My palms started to sweat, and I hadn't even swung my blade toward someone yet. My stomach revolted against the notion but what other choice did I have? This wasn't the time to get soft. I needed to be hard- like steel! I couldn't hesitate.

Another boom shook the earth and bucked the dirt underneath of my feet. I stumbled but kept upright and charging onwards. BOOM! BOOM! BOOM! I looked over as small fire bombs were catapulted from one of the towers of the castle down to the field. The ground felt like it was made of rubber as it bucked and turned from the explosions going off. I gritted my teeth and kept my eyes on the double doors of the castle where guards were slowly pouring out. Eye on the prize. Ignore the rest and keep pushing until you make it.

A guard charged at me from the bottom of the marbled steps. His blade was poised high for his strike. I lifted my own blade to meet him and in one hard strike- I was disarmed. The blade flew uselessly from my clammy finger tips and landed somewhere in the fray. I'm not a hero. I'm no warrior. I let out a high pitched, blood curdling sound and ran.

Thank Gods the guard was too stunned to stop me from shooting right past him and up the marbled steps. I literally threw myself into the doors- which hurt my shoulder again- and burst into the main hall like a psychopath.

My feet slipped on the smooth marble floors and I almost crashed into a rushing maid. She screamed, I screamed, we both ran in opposite directions. The heavy sounds of guards running through the halls made me dart into the closest room I could find. It was a large, and well-equipped kitchen.

Obviously, anyone who lived in the castle lived a life of luxury compared to the outside; but the set-up for the cooks was mind blowing. Six stoves! Five ovens! The pantry took up the right wall with wooden shelves stocked to the point of breaking. A massive stone table was set up in the middle of the room with bowls, cutting boards, baskets and skillets sitting on it. Above the table hung dozens of different sized, shaped, and colored pots and pans. Some were brilliantly designed while others made me scratch my head. A copper pot in the shape of a triangle. What purpose could that have?

"He ran this way!" someone shouted from down the hall. Panic had me in her cold, paralyzing hands. I couldn't think, I just reacted and grabbed a cast iron skillet from off the counter. When the door swung open, I brought it down on the first head that popped in. CLANG! The guard garbled something as he fell unconscious to the ground. I held my breath but another one didn't follow. A surge of hope raced through me. Turned out I was damn good at wielding my beloved pots and pans! Maybe a hero didn't need a sword after all. Maybe a hero just needed to be armed with something he was familiar with and filled with determination.

Goodbye fear and hello hidden strength!

"He's in the kitchen!"

Just kidding! I spun around and searched my surroundings for a good hiding place. Servant stairs would work. Tucking the long handle of the skillet into my belt, I dashed to the back of the kitchen and peeked up the narrow stairwell. It looked empty, and the pounding of heavy feet from behind propelled me forward. The stairwell spiraled upwards tightly, but I moved as quickly as the space and design allowed. The first door opened to a dark corner of the dining hall. The table in there put the stone one in the kitchen to shame. I swear that thing had to be close to a mile long with a cream runner draped down the center. I closed the door and kept ascending the stairs.

The second door led to a hallway filled with more guards whose backs were turned to me. Carefully I closed that door and quietly continued my search. The stairs ended at a third door, which I quietly and slowly pushed open. It was a vast bedroom with golden bed posts, wooden furnishings, and plush animal skin rugs. The windows took up an entire wall but were darkened with thick, red curtains. It was the most lavish bedroom I had ever been in. Tiptoeing across the floor, I crossed over to the other door. The knob was gold. Of course. I snapped out of my ogling and turned it. The long hallway outside was completely empty. Odd. And now I was lost.

Rich artwork adorned the walls and I had to remind myself that danger could be behind any corner and to focus on the task at hand. It took a few minutes, but I finally found a stone staircase that led up. This one echoed with the cries of those foul beasts that had stolen my donkey. I gripped my skillet and darted up the steps. This passage was as narrow as the servant's stairs but stopped at a thick iron gate. Beyond the gate, massive birds with wings like bats perched around a crude nest of straw. Their hooked beaks were longer than I first imagined. They were probably five feet long and attached to a circular head with narrowed black eyes.

Bones littered the ground, both animal and human shaped. But try as I might to find him, Gilbert was gone. I didn't even see so much as a tuft of his fur left behind. My eyes stung as my heart raced. No... It was supposed to be a few days before they ate. But then, we didn't know when they had their last meal before they stole my dearest friend from me. I took a step back and almost fell down the stairs.

No...

"Gilbert."

Yet, instead of being filled with a gut-wrenching sorrow, I was filled with something else. Rage. This vile piece of trash kept his people prisoner behind a barrier that was meant only to protect them from harm. He brought horrid creatures to life for his own sick amusement. He ripped apart families for gold. Destroyed innocents for his pleasure. And the worthless traitor killed my best friend.

He was going to pay.

CHAPTER TEN

MY GRIP ON the skillet tightened as I whirled around and descended the steps. Each step I took only made the fire inside of me grow hotter. When I walked back into the hall, two guards stood ready for me. Their blades glittered in the soft light, but cast iron is stronger than some fancy, over-stressed steel. We clashed with a symphony of deafening clangs. One guard lost his sword to my pan, the other tried to parry and snag my unprotected side. I danced to the left and swung down with my weapon. The iron connected with his wrist which cracked on the impact. His sword clattered to the ground uselessly as he howled in pain. Then I brought my weapon up in a brutal arc and connected with his forehead. He fell backwards and collapsed on the ground, unmoving save for a single tortured groan. One guard down.

The other of the duo was trying to collect his weapon. I sprinted down the hall behind me and jumped into the air, swinging my pan out like a club. He spun around in time to see the skillet meet his nose. Blood gushed out and sprayed the area. The guard cried out as he was thrown backwards and smashed his head on the hard floors.

My boots pounded down the hall, driven by a need to exact revenge for every lost soul that had to suffer under this tyranny. I found the main staircase and darted down it, meeting another group of guards head on. I bellowed out a war cry and swung madly at the group. Silver against black. The deadly duel blurred in front of me as I gave each swing everything I had. Pan to the back of one guy's head. Pan to the front of one guy's knee. I felt a vague sting in my left arm but ignored it to swing my weapon up into another guy's jaw. One by one, everyone fell unconscious around me.

It didn't take a genius to determine that the gold encrusted double doors nearly as tall as the high vaulted ceiling, adorned in jewels, with six guards standing at attention, protected the king. I rolled my wrists and charged forward. Six against one wasn't good odds. I may have anger and adrenaline fueling me, but about three seconds into the battle I realized my mistake. I wasn't trained as these men were. Their blades sliced into my pants and split open my leather vest. But then, I've never heard of a hero who didn't have friends.

Nyx-Ente roared as he jumped to my aid. I don't know when he got into the castle, but between the two of us, the odds were almost even. We pushed the guards back, taking two of them down quickly. Sweat dripped down my face and my arms ached but I dodged and retaliated with everything I had. An arrow zipped past my ear and landed in between the plates of armor on a man's arm. It sunk deeply into his arm pit, causing him to drop his weapon and fall to his knees with a shout of pain. Jorgon, the blond, swapped his bow for a short sword as he joined the battle. The sickening sound of steel slicing through flesh will never leave my dreams. Once the guards were down, we caught our breath and opened the doors.

The throne room was massive. It had to take up most of the first floor with hundreds of small torches lining the walls to illuminate such a monstrous waste of space. Thick columns rose up in rows of three on the left and right side, made from marble with golden veins running through them. The tapestries were all records of the new king as he stood over the masses with an orb raised high in his hands. And perched on his gilded throne in the very back, was the fat King in question who wore a smirk across his ugly face.

His right hand rested on top of a large orb that continuously changed color with swirls of thick smoke twisting violently inside. "Well, I can't say I didn't see this coming. Welcome to my humble home," he cackled and made an extravagant gesture with his left hand.

I widened my stance and thrusted out my pan, "cut the crap, it's time to end this."

"GUARDS!"

We rushed forward as a string of guards poured out from hidden passageways behind the throne. With our grips steady on our weapons, we met them in the middle of the room. The clang of steel echoed but our momentum forward was halted as the numbers against us kept adding in. Thankfully, the odds didn't last long. Comrades filed in from the doorway, screaming as they engaged in battle and attempted to push the opposing forces back. King Hosaku watched the scene unfold before him for a minute or two before quietly standing and tucking the large orb within his robes. He then made for the passages behind the throne.

"Curse you!" I cried out as I pushed into the guards in front of me, hoping there would be enough of a break to fit through. There wasn't. The slimy crook was going to get away. Even Aasgard whose broad sword was as long and thick as the average man couldn't carve a path through the thick wall of armored bodies protecting King Hosaku. From the sides we were losing our ground and the guards slipped in to surround our small army. Healers screamed their chants above the breaking bones of war but the few we had on our side couldn't keep up with the damage being inflicted on us.

Just as I was beginning to lose hope, a loud bray lifted my heart up with joy. I turned my head and watched as a gallant donkey galloped into the room with his teeth bared. He kicked out with his hindlegs and tossed a guard back into the hallway outside.

"Oh Gods, is it really you?" I nearly sobbed. "GILBERT!"

My fiercely loyal companion rushed to my side, slowing only enough for me to climb onto his back. I swallowed against the tidal wave of emotion that threated to consume me and gently dug my heels into his sides.

"After that king!"

The guards started to scramble apart as Gilbert charged forward. I held on tightly while we bucked our way to the throne, just in time to watch the king take the first step down into a hidden stairwell. I dug my heels into Gilberts sides again. "HE-YAH!"

We crashed straight into his back, tumbling as one crazy blob of flailing limbs down into the room below. Something cracked, someone screamed, and then we finally collided with the floor at the end.

The room was a twisted mix of laboratory and dungeon. The floors and walls were made of hard slabs of stone. Behind me were rows of cages made from stone, steel, and god only knows what the black pieces were scattered between the bricks. It was too dark to see what was kept inside of them, but the sounds were something straight out of a nightmare.

Something gurgled with a low, pained moan.

Another snarled like a wolf but then hissed like a viper. Several small creatures shrieked and threw themselves at the bars that rattled and clanked. Crude symbols were painted in some type of purplish paint above each door, but I couldn't read the language they were written in. If it was even a language at all...

I turned my head to check on Gilbert who was already climbing to his hooves. The stubborn old mule appeared to be fine. Thank the Gods again...

The far part of the room was lined with shelves of thousands of books, scrolls, and jars filled with mysterious liquids. It had tables lined neatly in rows of two with some intimidating tools resting on their hard surfaces. The thing that creeped me out the most was a wooden chair with leather straps nailed into the arms and legs.

The king groaned and slowly rolled onto his feet, pushing me to get up as well. The orb he had been carrying was across the room by one of the cages. I cringed knowing that I needed to retrieve it, and in doing so would come face to face with whatever monster laid inside.

My skillet had skittered over by the tables, so I considered it lost and braced myself for hand to hand combat. I didn't know how to throw a punch or pull off any fancy kicks, but I was going to do my best to keep this horrid man from terrorizing this kingdom any longer.

As I moved a step towards the orb, the injuries I sustained roared to life with a vengeance. The tidal wave of agony dropped me to my knees with a harsh gasp. A rib felt cracked, my shoulder was bleeding profusely from a blade I hadn't dodged, shallower cuts on my chest and abdomen stung, and my legs felt like they were made from jelly. I started to sweat as I grasped at my wounded arm.

The king watched me struggle with a wide smile. "Oh, how the mighty hero falls," he taunted as he stepped around me. "Tell me, was this all worth it? Hmm?"

"Not yet," I gasped out, slowly pushing myself up. "But it will be once you're gone."

"Such brave words for a man two feet away from death's warm embrace."

I snapped my head at him as the room began to hum with energy. His eyes danced with glee as he raised his hands. "You didn't believe my magic was contained to a single vessel, did you?"

No, but I had kind of hoped so...

Gilbert let out a nervous bray and backed away from King Hosaku as the energy pulsed harder. It was becoming a tangible thing, snapping and sparking in the air. I gritted my teeth as I lunged at the source, but the spell was cemented and struck back. Lightning shot out from his raised palms and slammed straight into my chest. I screamed as the bolts coursed through my veins, working my muscles against my own demands and frying my bones. It threw me back onto the stone floor several feet away from where the King cackled with joy. The room faded in and out of my consciousness as I groaned and tried to move. I couldn't.

"You tried hard, I'll give you that. But you're no great hero, boy. You're just a lowly pots and pans salesmen who let a group of traitors get into your head. I would feel bad if you weren't so useless."

I fought against the need to sleep. "Why?" I gasped out, tossing my head back and forth to shake myself back into reality, "Why are you doing this?"

"Why?" He repeated thoughtfully, "well that's simple. I want them to hurt as badly as I did when I was barred from my own home lands."

Slowly my muscles began to respond to me again. Just one finger twitched but it sparked a new hope that was quickly growing into a warm fire inside my heart. "What?"

"During the war, the barrier was erected to protect the citizens from being destroyed by the larger opposing forces," the king stated as he slowly started to pace in front of the cages. "It prevented anyone outside from coming in, including young lads travelling with their parents to visit extended family. This kingdom was my home and they turned their backs on us! Instead of fighting, they cowardly hid away from the world while I watched my parents die by the hands of the dwarves!

I survived, though, and when the war ended and the barrier was dropped, I jumped at my chance to exact my revenge. Now, a new war has started and none of the precious little peasants can hide any longer."

The effects of the lightning finally ended and sprung back up to my feet. I almost felt bad for him until he decided that killing more innocents somehow righted a wrong.

King Hosaku let out a low growl, the orb was already back in his hands, but it had a small crack in its surface that I hadn't noticed earlier. It tumbled down stone steps into a stone room, and only cracked a tiny bit? What would it take to break this thing?!

Gilbert let out an enraged bray as he charged towards the King, but the spell lashed out again and slammed straight into my best friend. "Nooo! Gilbert!" I cried out as he was thrown across the room. His body landed with a heavy thud. He twitched a few times, then went limp.

Terror tried to seize me in her cold hands, but I fought it. The same as I fought the effects of the magic still buzzing in my veins. I fought the doubt. I fought the pain. I fought everything, and I stood back up.

"But you know what? I'm not going to just lay down and accept death either. Anyone can become a hero if they're just brave enough to try!"

I was ready this time as he raised his palm again and sent a stream of lightning arching across the room.

I jumped to the left, rolling back to my knees by the tables and that awful chair device.

"HEROS ARE JUST A FAIRYTALE! IT'S TIME FOR YOU TO GROW UP!" The King roared as the magic in the air shifted. A soft wind blew around the open space, warm but slowly growing hotter with each second.

"No!" I snapped back as I rose to my feet. "A hero is someone who never gives up, even when they're scared out of their mind and have everything to lose!"

He swung his arm outwards like he was slapping me from afar. A sudden gust of sweltering wind smashed into my abdomen and threw me back into the lines of shelves adorning the wall. Jars broke, books fell, and wood splintered as my back crushed into it. The wind disappeared as I gasped for breath and dropped suddenly to the floor again. The stone smarted against my already bruised knees and god only knows what was raining down on my head. Some of it burned, some of it felt cold like rain, and the others smelled worse than a skunkbear.

I wiped the liquid from my face and glared at my opponent. "You keep saying you're going to win because I'm just a pots and pans salesman. That might be true, but that's why I want to become a hero. In every story I've ever heard growing up, the hero always wins. You need to be stopped, this ruthless ruling must end or else this kingdom will fall to dust! That's why

I want to be a hero. I want to see this kingdom come alive again! I don't want any more people to die!"

Amid the chaos was a familiar clanging sound that kept my hope burning brighter. I could still do this. I had to do this. Everyone upstairs was doing their part to become heroes of this kingdom. It was time I joined their honorable ranks. Today, I become a hero!

CHAPTER·ELEVEN

THANKS TO THAT gust of wind, I had my trusty skillet back. I gripped its cool handle and rose back to my feet. I had to get close to hit him, which meant guessing his attacks better. I didn't know a lot about magic, but I knew from the last two hits that it took a moment to charge. And all magic had limits.

I heard an angry snort and watched Gilbert lift his head from the corner of my eye. Relief swept through me for a moment, but then quickly died. He wouldn't be truly safe until King Hosaku was stopped. This battle needed to end soon.

Another deafening BOOM shook the foundation of the castle. Dust and pebbles rained down on us as tiny cracks appeared in the surface of the ceiling. King Hosaku looked up in confusion, and I used the opportunity to charge towards him. His attention snapped back at me and that humming energy built up again. Seven feet away and he lifted his palm up.

I threw myself to the left to avoid the electricity that blasted the ground.

A heat wave blasted through the room. Fire? I swallowed hard and started bouncing on my heels with my gaze fixed steadily on The Traitor. I started to sweat from the building inferno and my own fear. Finally, the King moved, and so did I. He thrust his fist out towards me and I ran to the right. His fist followed me, the air still pulsing with the weight of his magic as the fire blast swept out and licked the back of my heels. I bit my bottom lip against the hiss of pain and pushed myself to keep going. The wall was coming up quick. Praying that the spell was short lived like the others, I dropped to my knees and bent back as far as I could, so my shoulders and back were pressed against my aching feet and the cool floor.

The column of flames swept past my face, heating the skin but moved over my body without touching my delicate flesh. Then the fire vanished as the magic ran out. I let out a breath of relief and lifted myself up again in one fluent movement.

I spun back to face the row of cages I was slowly getting closer to and tightened my grip on the handle of my weapon. The King let out a bellow of frustration. The swirling smoke in the orb started moving more erratically and turned into a black darker than midnight. King Hosaku gripped the orb with both hands and thrust it out in front of him.

"I won't be toyed with by a lowly blacksmith! DIE ALREADY!" he screamed.

"Not today."

The room was lit up with a bright yellow circle on the ground. Letters, symbols, and strange lines formed within it with each step I took. The energy shifted, becoming something utterly terrifying and strange. It was heavy like molasses, sapping at my strength as I pushed myself to keep going. Closer… Closer… I was almost within range of the King, but the magic was wrapping around my body and trying to pull it down.

Hooves thundered behind me, and I reached out blindly with my free hand while crying out for help. Fur filled my palm and a bray echoed in my ears. I gripped it tightly and used my friend's help to find my feet again. He pushed his body against my own and forced me onto his back. I could see the magic literally lifting from the circle and attacking his legs with its yellow vined arms. But Gilbert didn't slow down. He bunched up his hindlegs and jumped into the air, over the edge of the circle, and straight at the King whose eyes grew wider than the orb he carried.

He attempted to move out of the way. He made it two steps to the side before we arched downwards, and the tips of Gilberts hooves touched the floor again. I swung my pan out like a baseball bat, smashing it right into the front of the orb. Over that stupid, taunting tiny crack. And when the sounds of glass shattering touched my ears, I finally allowed myself to smile. Now I would let myself believe that I was capable of being a hero.

The magic carefully contained inside the glass ball exploded free. It sent everyone and everything nearby flying across the room. Again. Not fun when you're riding a donkey and suddenly find his seriously heavy body crushing down on yours. The explosion shook the entire room, bending and breaking the bars of the cages that had kept the mysterious creatures captive and completely smashing anything made weaker than wood.

The circle in the room merely faded out into nothingness, and when the magic finally left, the air lifted. I coughed from the dust that was kicked up and struggled underneath Gilbert's large frame. "Up... Boy," I grunted. He brayed what I'm assuming was an apology and climbed to his hooves to move away from me. I groaned at the sudden freedom my numb limbs felt. Breath one... two... three... four...

With a groan I pushed myself up into a sitting position and held my throbbing head. Was it finally over? Could this day blessedly end already? I flexed my other hand around the handle of my bent pan that somehow, I managed to keep during the whole mess as the room tilted and swayed.

A low snarl sent a shiver down my spine. That would be a big, fat, no.

I blinked twice to clear my vision of little black dots

and squinted at the beasts slowly emerging from their cages. Some appeared to be big cats but had elongated fangs that reached the bottom of their jaws and wings sprouting from their backs. Two others may have been wolves at some point but were twisted to stand on two legs with claws five inches long with tusks of a boar and covered in matted, black... I wanted to call it slime. It definitely didn't resemble fur and defied all rules of gravity and logic as it stuck to their skin.

The shrieks stepped into the light and I had to swallow against the urge to vomit. They were animated skeletons of small monkeys- some still had pieces of rotting flesh stuck to their bones. They rattled as they moved with an unnatural blue fire burning in their eye sockets. I hadn't believed necromancy was a real power until this moment. Now I realized how messed up the dark magic was. Although the skeletons were only knee high, they easily beat every other creature on the scary meter. I never wanted to see anything like it again.

The creatures' attentions were fixed on King Hosaku. They approached him slowly as if they had all the time in the world and knew he wouldn't be able to escape. Finally, that horrid man looked terrified. He crawled backwards with one hand thrusted out in front of him. "D-don't you dare! I created you! Listen to me! Go b-back to your cells!"

The beasts ignored his desperate rantings and

continued advancing on him. His back hit the wall and the room crackled with more energy. "I will destroy you all!" he roared, unleashing another powerful lightning attack outwards. The creatures didn't pause as the electricity coursed through their bodies and ripped through their... flesh? Can you even call it that on some of the things that were brought to life?

Semantics aside, I wasn't going to keep hanging out with things that weren't affected by lightning. I turned to Gilbert, who looked just as scared and confused as I was and climbed onto his back. I dug my heels into his sides and whispered, "let's get out of here boy."

I was only spared a glance or two from some of the creatures as we bolted for the stairs. I kept my eyes locked forward as the growls rumbled through the room and the King started screaming. Gilbert climbed the steps quickly, with the light at the end of the tunnel our shining beacon of freedom. We soared through the entrance just as the wet sounds of feasting started.

I yanked Gilbert to a stop only a few steps on the marbled floor of the throne room and threw myself off his back. I landed on shaky knees and stumbled into the side of the throne, which is where I decided to lean over and empty the contents of my stomach. I doubted the new King would want to use the throne that Hosaku had sat his large butt on for so long, but I was certain, after I was done gagging, that it was going to be burned no matter what the new royalty thought.

Slowly I lifted my face to look out at the crowd staring at me with a mix of sympathy, horror, disgust, and understanding. The guards that hadn't been killed in battle were tied up with thick pieces of rope and pushed to the sides of the room with a few of our own members to keep watch over them. The others were grouped together as if they were discussing something that I had interrupted.

Aasgard and Nyx-Ente were the ones who looked at me with understanding. Nyx-Ente started to approach the base of the throne, when a series of loud shrieks echoes up from the hidden stairway. I shivered and pointed to the door behind me. "We have to seal that tunnel up! We can't let those things escape!"

Aasgard nodded and spun around to address the crowd. "Well? You heard him! Board up that tunnel! Bring whatever you can find!"

The army moved immediately with more commands barked out to bring the enchanters forward. I tuned it out as Gilbert nudged me carefully and snorted softly. I smiled weakly and stroked his nose, the strength slowly returning to my body. He nuzzled the side of my face gently, then backed away as Aasgard cleared his throat.

"Want to tell us what happened back there?" he inquired, as five large men lugged one of the golden throne room doors up the steps of the tunnel entrance. I watched them groan and huff as they pushed the door against the wall as tightly as they could, while a mage conjured small blue flames to his fingertips. I wasn't sure a wielded makeshift door would hold forever, but it worked for now.

"I fought against the king, only for him to be killed by his own need for revenge."

Aasgard nodded and offered me a canteen of water to sip on. "Are you going to be alright?"

"Physically? I think I'll be fine..."

Nyx-Ente's face darkened as he moved closer, "it isn't called war because it's good for a man's soul. War does things to a person that nothing else can compare to. It's fine to admit ya aren't okay."

Gilbert stomped his hoof and snorted as if he agreed. I bit my bottom lip and attempted to stand up straighter, to hold myself as high as I should be feeling right now. The terrified last screams of the king rang through the room and I realized he was right. I wasn't okay. I wanted, more than anything, to yank the magic users back and break open the temporary door. I wanted to save a man that deserved everything he got.

My eyes stung as I looked back up at Aasard and Nyx-Ente and asked, "what makes a man different than the king? What stops you from becoming a ruthless murderer? At what point does it become enough?"

"Do you want to kill us? Do you want to overthrow another city, or kingdom, and take on that throne while laughing at the blood-stained walls?" Aasgard asked quietly.

My horrified expression must have been enough, because he nodded and continued.

"That is what stops someone from becoming a ruthless tyrant. It is what lies in your heart that leads you. You, Sir Paul Paulson, have a good and pure heart. This war won't change that."

Aasgard paused again to look back out at the battered and bloody faces of our group. They stared back, some from the ground where they laid to have their injuries tended to and others from their feet which swayed with the effort to continue standing. They looked worse for wear, but their eyes still showed that hope that he had when I first fell into their ranks; and, for the first time, relief that the horror had finally ended.

"We have overcome a great deal today but that hope, that peace within our people- that is enough." Aasgard stated.

"Aye, and I think this is enough for today." Nyx-Ente grunted, giving me a hardy pat on the back.

I cracked a small smile, "and what about tomorrow?"

"Tomorrow can wait until morning. For now, let's celebrate our freedom and enjoy the beautiful possibilities we now have for a future!"

That I could do. Freedom comes with a heavy price that must be paid in full, but once the debt was taken care of, the rest was worth more than any precious gold. Now these people had a chance to regain their happiness. They could build their cities again and find families to live out the rest of their lives with. And me? Heck, I could probably do the same thing. But I would focus on the details later. For now, just being alive with my donkey was enough.

THE END

ABOUT THE AUTHOR

C.R. Garmen developed her passion for writing at a young age. Starting with retelling the story of three little pigs, she went on to dream of being an author one day. Born and raised in the suburbs of Detroit, she is very close to her family, especially her younger siblings who light up her world and continue to support and fuel her passion for telling stories. Jack of all trades, master of none; C.R. Garmen dabbles in every genre, finding that each one is just a new challenge to explore and take on.

Follow her on Facebook for more updates about
The World of Pallam, and other works in progress.
WWW.FACEBOOK.COM/CRGARMEN
And check out her blog for some exclusive interviews,
new releases, and more!
WWW.CRGARMEN.WORDPRESS.COM

www.ingramcontent.com/pod-product-compliance
Lightning Source LLC
Chambersburg PA
CBHW020618130626
46552CB00003B/1027